WAITING FOR THE

Waves

Michelle Nkamankeng

Illustrated by Megan Venter
Inspired by Sheena Nkamankeng

Published by LANSM Events Management & Services (Pty) Ltd

ISBN 978-0-620-73747-0

Cover Design by Lawrence Symonds

Illustrations by Megan Venter

Editing by Ink Imp

Additional desigh by Tarryn George

Printed and bound by CreateSpace

www.facebook.com/MichelleNkamankeng

youtube.com/MichelleNkamankeng

Twitter: @michelle_n23

michellenkamankeng@gmail.com

www.michellenkamankeng.com

Author's signature:

This book belongs to:

Contents

Acknowledgements

Firstly I would like to thank Almighty God for giving me the strength and knowledge to write this book. I also want to thank my team, and especially my mom, dad, and sister, for their support. Also thanks to everyone who made it possible for this book to be published.

Dedication

This book was written with passion
for my family.

I hope you like this story.
Have fun!

Yours,
Michelle Nkamankeng

Foreword

It is a great honour to write the foreword for a book by one of the pupils of Sacred Heart College.

Our children have to be taught that they are growing up in a world in which nothing is handed to you on a platter.

The jobs that their grandparents and parents have done do not exist anymore. For a child to believe in their own ability to create something that can bring pleasure to others and make a mark in the world, something that is the fruit of their own efforts, the product of agency and creativity, is remarkable. I remember taking my daughter, when she was small, to swim, to jump in the waves, to ride on tubes, and reading this brings with it feelings of nostalgia from those occasions.

But central to this story is the courage of Titi and the message that Michelle wants to give to young readers: if you want to, you can do anything. I do not believe that age should dictate what people are capable of; I encourage readers to judge Michelle's work on the content and enjoyment they get from it.

I love being able to work in a school that creates opportunities for children to express themselves and share that expression with the rest of the world.

Colin Northmore
Head of Sacred Heart College
Johannesburg, South Africa

This is the story of a little girl named Titi.

Titi lives with her family in a beautiful house next to a big beach. She loves the beach and the big blue ocean. So she spends most of her time at the beach, sometimes waiting for the waves or just swimming.

Titi will swim and swim and swim. She never gets tired. She just loves the big waves at the beach.

"How I wish I knew where these big waves are coming from," she will often think aloud.

The Big Pool

Close to the beach is a big hotel with a big pool. The pool is called "London".
Next to the big pool is a big water slide c alled "Tubesi".

Titi spends most of her time either sitting on the sand and waiting for the big waves or in front of the pool watching the hotel guests come and go.

On this very sunny day she gets so bored, she says to herself, "I am going to go on one of the water slides. It must be more fun than just sitting here and waiting for the waves."

So off she runs to the biggest water slides. Uncle Joe, who is looking after her today, sees Titi running to the water slide. Because he is so scared that she could hurt herself, he struggles to his feet and runs after her.

"Oh my gosh! She is running to the water slide alone," Uncle Joe says to himself looking worried.

"I can't let her go all by herself."

"Can someone please go after her?" He calls after Titi in his loud and speaking voice, still struggling to get on his feet so he can run after her.

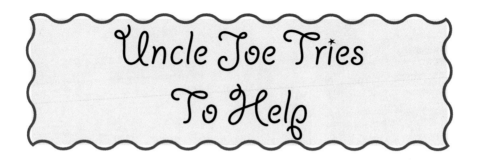

Uncle Joe Tries To Help

"Titi, Titi!" he calls after her. But Titi has gone
.

"Oh dear, I am just an old man, but I can't let
her go. I have to make sure that she is alright.
I promised her parents I will look after her,"
Uncle Joe complains in his weak and troubled
voice as he tries to run after Titi.

Finally Uncle Joe finds Titi standing in line for her turn on the slide. She is so excited when she sees him coming after her.

"Uncle Joe, see, only two more people to go until it's my turn," she says, jumping excitedly and waving at him.

"Young girl, I am out of breath," says Uncle Joe, panting as he tries to catch up with Titi.

"I am so excited Uncle Joe!" Titi waves as she impatiently gets ready to take her turn on the slide.

Seeing Titi so excited, Uncle Joe has the feeling she will explode for joy by the time she gets to the front of the line.

So he makes up his mind it will be more fun to join Titi. Then he takes off his shoes and shirt ready to join Titi in the line.

"Titi, wait for me," he shouts excitedly, waving to her.

Happily they find swimming tubes that are exactly their sizes.

They both put on the tubes and SWISH SWOOSH they slide through the tube and land in the fresh blue water of the big pool.

"Hahahahahaha," laugh Titi and Uncle Joe happily as they drag themselves out of the warm water of the pool.

"That was great fun," says Uncle Joe, looking at Titi.

"Let's do another round Uncle Joe, pleeeease," begs Titi.

"Ok, ok young woman," replies Uncle Joe, breathing hard.

"Yessssss, cool," laughs Titi. They take the same tube and run laughingly to the dark hole at the top of the next and much bigger water slide.

Uncle Joe sees that Titi's body is shaking.

He is not sure whether she is shaking with fear or excitement.

"Ha! Ha! Ha!" laughs Uncle Joe.

"I am just joking. You will land in the same fresh water that we landed in before," he explains.

"Calm down Titi. You will land in the same fresh water that we landed in before," he repeats, still laughing.

"You are so mean, Uncle Joe!" Titi shouts, pushing Uncle Joe aside and moving ahead to stand in front of him so she is the first to get on the slide.

Then it is her turn again.

Uncle Joe and Titi put the tubes over their heads again.

"Ready?" she asks, turning to look at Uncle Joe.

"Ready," Uncle Joe replies smiling.

Happily they take their seat at the entrance of the tube and SWISH SWOSH they slide through the big tube, down into the fresh blue water again.

With a big SPLASH they land in the fresh, blue warm water again laughing happily.

"Come Uncle Joe, let us swim another round in the fresh blue water." Titi begins swimming ahead of Uncle Joe with a big smile on her face.

"Great idea Titi," replies Uncle Joe as he swims after her.

"Catch me if you can Uncle Joe," Titi calls out as she swims faster to the other end of the pool with Joe chasing after her.

"Wait for me, Titi," he calls, out of breath.

"I can't swim as fast as you do, young woman."

Titi and Uncle Joe end up swimming many more rounds on the fresh blue water, having fun and enjoying themselves.

"Look, Uncle Joe!" Titi suddenly shouts, pointing at the big blue ocean. "The big wave, the big wave," she shouts excitedly, going out of the water and running towards the ocean.

The Big Wave

"Uncle Joe, the big wave, see over there," she says, pointing at the ocean. "Is it coming our way, Uncle Joe?" Titi looks at him, frightened.

Because she is too scared, she moves backward, turns around and runs back to Uncle Joe. At the same time she notices the rest of her family, her mom, dad, her two sisters and her brother, coming towards her, just in time to see the big wave too.

"I can't stand the big wave," Titi says, grabbing Uncle Joe's hand. "What? You can't stand this? You love the waves. You have been waiting for the BIG WAVE all day long," Uncle Joe replies laughing as he takes Titi's hand.

"Come on Titi! You are the bravest little girl I know in the whole world," he says. Uncle Joe is trying to comfort her.

Titi looks at Uncle Joe and smiles.

"Really, Uncle Joe? Am I really the bravest girl you know?" she asks, looking at her Uncle Joe with her big eyes.

Uncle Joe nods his head. "Yes, you are the bravest little girl I know. You are my bravest Titi," he says as he hugs her.

"I will be brave, Uncle Joe," Titi says, freeing herself from Uncle Joe's arms and going carefully closer to the big wave.

"If you are scared, remember I am with you and nothing can happen to you as long as I am with you," says Uncle Joe.

"Off you go. Go watch the BIG WAVE you have been waiting for," he says as he watches her go.

Titi is still a little afraid, so she looks up to Uncle Joe.

"I want you to come with me, Uncle Joe, please come with me."

Titi grabs her uncle's hand tightly looking him straight in the eye.

Together they run towards the ocean as the rest of the family cheers them on.

"Onward, forward you go, Titi," they say.

Titi is so freaked out as she runs towards the ocean with Uncle Joe. As they come closer to the big waves, Uncle Joe speaks to Titi.

"Come on Titi, you can do this, brave girl." Titi dips her feet in the cold water of the ocean. It feels so cold and she loves it.

"Look Uncle Joe, the wave has gone!" she says pointing to the water.

The Bravest Girl In The Whole World

"Oh yes, we made it just in time to see the big waves."

"Yes we made it, we made it and I was not afraid," Titi shouts, jumping in front of Uncle Joe. "I made it, I am the bravest girl in the whole world. I made it!" Titi is so happy.

The waiting for the BIG WAVE is now over.

"Come Uncle Joe, let us go again into the dark hole. Let us slide down into the fresh blue water again to celebrate the BIG WAVES," she begs.

"No! No! No! I have something else to do now," says Uncle Joe.

"Come, take your tube and go ahead, I
will come after you."

"Ok" said Titi, "I am ready. Let's go".

And off she goes, with Uncle Joe after her. They get to the big slippery slide.

"Go ahead, Titi, go first."

"I can't do this, Uncle Joe."

"Come on. Remember you are the bravest girl I know in the whole world and you did it before."

"Ok, here I go," and off Titi goes.

"Weeeeee!" She shouts as she goes SPISH SPLOSH in the big tube.

Uncle Joe is more proud of Titi than he has ever been before in his life. As both of them join the family afterwards, Titi tells the whole story about what happened.

"Are you still scared of the BIG WAVE, Titi?" her mum asked.

"No, I am not scared of the BIG WAVES anymore, mum," she answers proudly.

"Cool, Titi... Oh look, there is another big wave coming. Do you want to go and see it?" her mum asks pointing to the ocean.

"Oh yes, oh yes," says Titi. "Mum, see, I am doing this all alone this time," and off she goes again, this time alone.

Laughing, she runs towards the big ocean, stopping where she can see the big waves as they disappear in the sand on the beach.

"SWISH!" she says as the wave dies in front of her.

"SWOOSH! WEEEE!" Titi shouts happily as she runs back to her family. Happily they go back home.

Since then Titi and her family have lived in their home not far from the beach.

Then Titi decided to write a book called "Waiting for the Waves," which is the book you just read!

Titi busy writing the book
"Waiting for the Waves"

Titi and her family reading the book
"Waiting for the Waves"

Titi and sister reading the book to the church.

Titi presenting the book to the school.

Watch this space, more books to come!

Made in the USA
Las Vegas, NV
07 July 2023

74351845R00036